HANUMAN

THE FLYING HERO

HANUMAN
THE FLYING HERO

Sudhamahi Regunathan
Illustrated by Anushka Madhavan

BLOOMSBURY
NEW DELHI • LONDON • OXFORD • NEW YORK • SYDNEY

BLOOMSBURY INDIA
Bloomsbury Publishing India Pvt. Ltd
Second Floor, LSC Building No. 4, DDA Complex, Pocket C – 6 & 7,
Vasant Kunj, New Delhi, 110070

BLOOMSBURY, BLOOMSBURY INDIA and the Diana logo are trademarks of Bloomsbury Publishing Plc

First published in India 2025

ISBN: 978-93-61313-12-7; eBook: 978-93-61316-10-4

2 4 6 8 10 9 7 5 3 1

Design by Anushka Madhavan
Printed and bound in India by Thomson Press

FSC www.fsc.org MIX Paper | Supporting responsible forestry FSC® C010615

To Kanina, Lila, Raaga, Rhta, Viren and Samarth, my little teachers

Contents

HOW HANUMAN GOT HIS NAME

On a mountain high
Among rivers and trees
Lived a little child
Who was as **HAPPY** as can be.

His mother was Anjana
His father, the mighty God of Wind
Who blows the world over
The air that we all breathe in.

'tweet'
'cheep-cheep'
'tweet-tweet'

One day, the child felt hungry
'Let me get you a fruit,' said Mummy
She walked to the orchard
To choose from the ripe and luscious many.

'Oh! Don't you bother, Mummy
That is the fruit I want
THAT BRIGHT, RIPE, ORANGE FRUIT
Looks juicy and sweet to me.'

Off went the child
With a leap and a jump
He began to **FLY**
Soaring into the sky.

'That is not a fruit, my child
It is the Sun,' Mummy was saying
But he had flown away
He was no longer there to hear.

'He is flying,' exclaimed his mummy
Stunned and shocked
'Come back, my child, come back
It is not safe to fly so high.'

The brilliant Sun watched from above
'What a wondrous sight,' he cried
'A little child, so strong and brave
Is flying through the sky!'

Many a star and planet, too, saw
The amazing sight of a child in flight
'I will look at his face,' said one planet
And stepped out of its orbit fixed.

'Am I lucky!' exclaimed the little child
'Another fruit have I found
Closer to me as this one is
I WILL EAT IT FIRST, I say!'

Seeing the child come towards it
The planet, **TERRIFIED, RAN**
As fast as it could to the house of Indra,
The King of the Skies, and knocked urgently at his door.

'A child is chasing us, Lord Indra
Save us from his flight
Now he is headed towards the Sun
Save us from his might.'

'noo!'
'Ohh noo'
'SAVVEE USS!'

Looking out of his window, Lord Indra found
A brave young child racing to the Sun
Indra aimed his thunderbolt at him
To stop him on his flight along the sky.

Oh! **THE THUNDERBOLT HIT THE CHILD ON HIS CHIN**
And down he tumbled, swirling as he fell
'My son,' cried the Wind God as he saw
The poor little child in free fall.

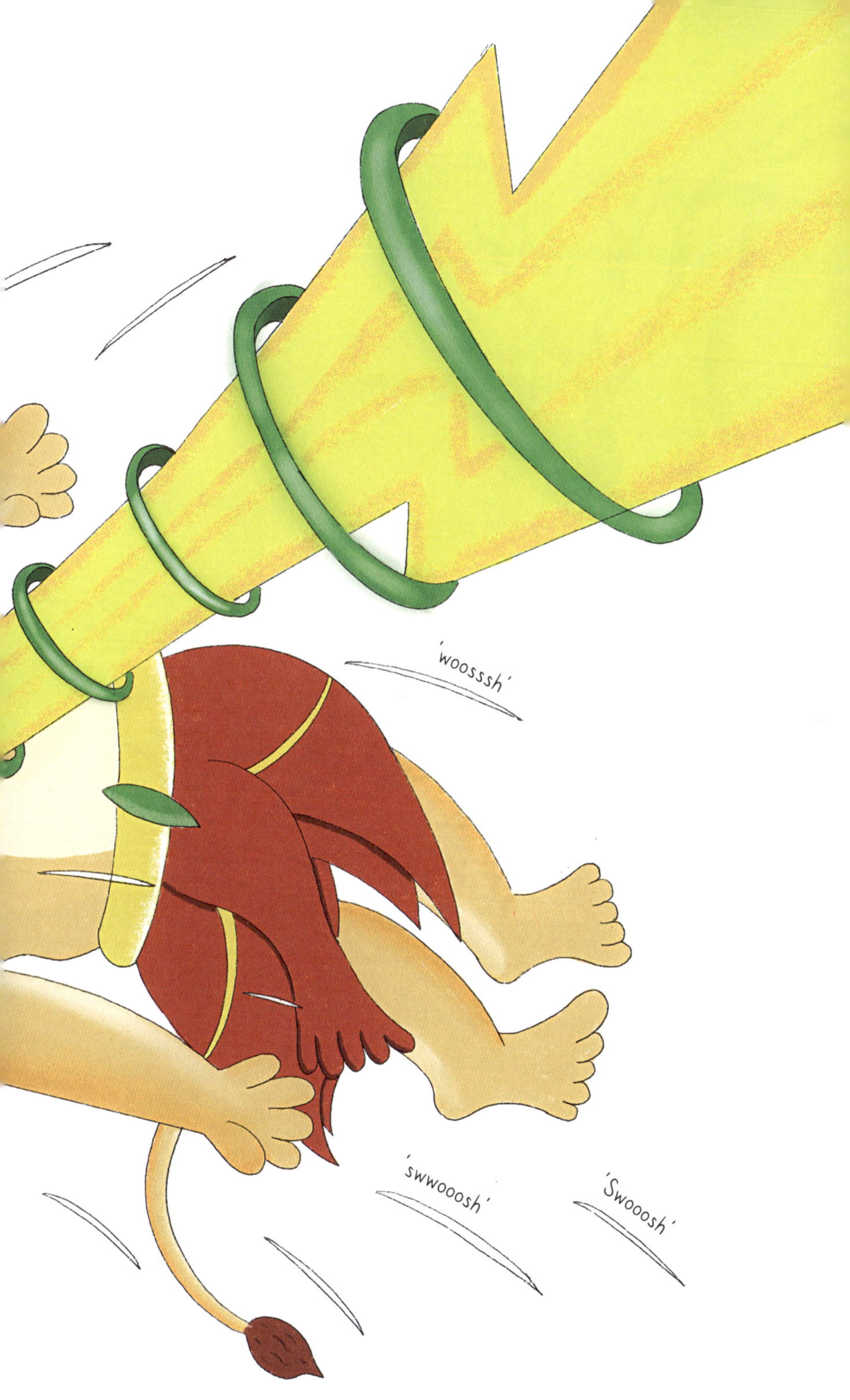
'woossssh'
'swwooosh'
'Swooosh'

'sigh'
'sigh'

Full of anger, the Wind God said,
'I will sit still and not blow any more.'
Applying a balm on his son's chin
He held the little one in his arms.

When the wind stopped blowing
THERE WAS NO AIR TO BREATHE
'We will all perish,' cried the people
Animals, birds and trees alike.

'Oh God, save us please,' they prayed
'We need air to breathe
Calm down the Wind God
Or else we will not remain alive.'

Whoooooooooooooooooooooooooooooooooooooooo

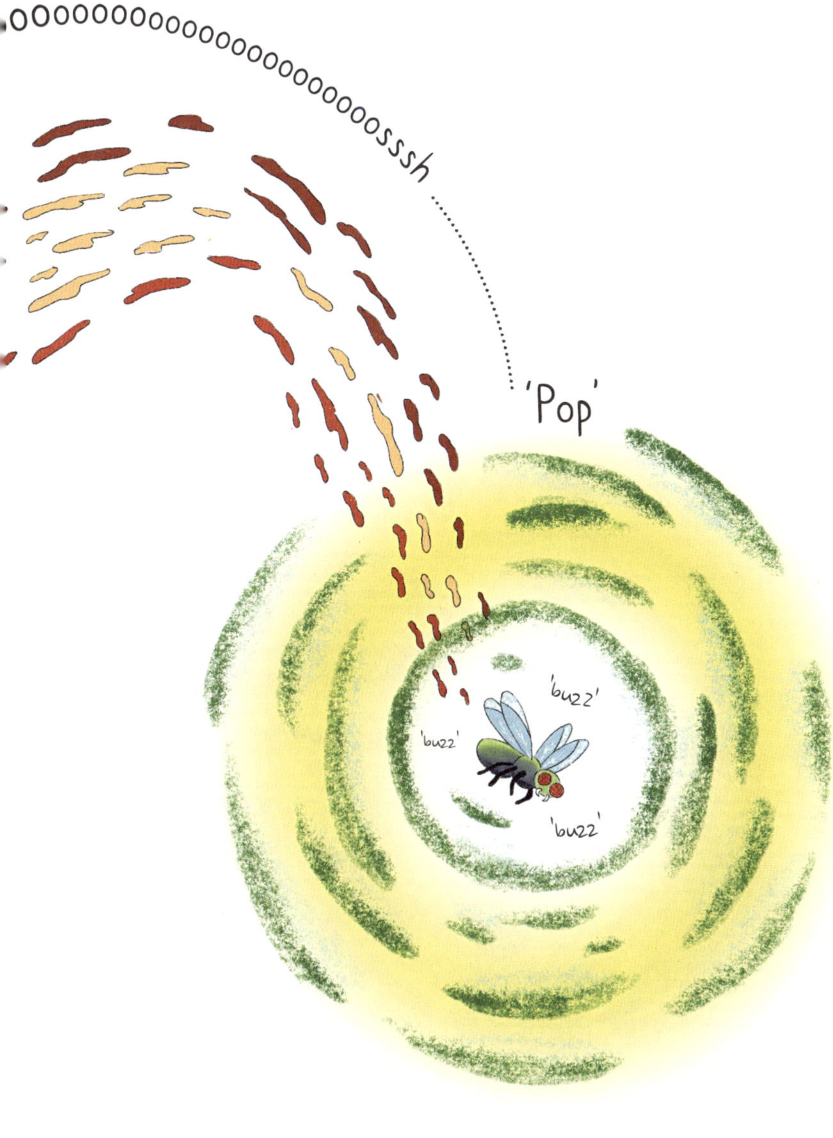

Brahma, the creator of the Universe, was the first to arrive

'Bless him, all you gods,' he ordered

'I grant him the power to change his form

A MAN, A MONKEY, A FLY, A GIANT

He can choose to be at will.'

Indra came flying down next
Picking up the child in his arms
He soothed him with loving words
'My thunderbolt can never harm you again.'

'You have got hurt on your "**HANU**"
Which is Sanskrit for chin
So from now on, as **HANUMAN** you will be known
Greater than the greatest, stronger than the strongest.'

'I wish him well too,' said the Sun
Sad as it was to see Hanuman fall
'I'll share with you my **BRIGHTNESS**, Hanuman
And you too will speak wisely and well.'

'I watched you as you flew over me,'
Said the Lord of the Oceans
'You will live very long
Full of **HEALTH** and **GOOD CHEER**.'

'My son will be as **SWIFT** as me,'
Said the Wind God, father of the child
And then many others came along too
To **GIVE MORE POWERS TO HANUMAN.**

And so it was that Hanuman got his **NAME**
And so it was that his strength he got
So it was that he got his **POWER**, his **SPEED**
INTELLIGENCE, COURAGE, FAME and all.

'WISE HANUMAN'
'POWERFUL HANUMAN'
'MIGHTY HANUMAN'

HOW HANUMAN CROSSED THE SEA

Prince Rama was walking with his brother Lakshmana
When Hanuman met him in the forest one day
'What a wonderful man he looks like!' thought Hanuman
'I wish I could be near him always.'

'Greetings!' said Hanuman to Rama
'What brings you here, dear sir?'
'**MY WIFE, SITA, I CANNOT FIND**,' replied Rama
'In search of her we have come this way.'

'And who are you, who meets us here?'
Asked Rama and Lakshmana
'My name is Hanuman and I serve
My king, the good-natured and loyal Sugriva.'

'Sugriva will support you,' promised Hanuman
And took the brothers up a hill close by
Where Rama met King Surgiva and asked, 'Will you help me
Find Sita with your large army of brave monkeys and bears?'

All the monkeys straightened their tails
And along with the bears folded their hands
'Sure, Lord Rama, we will go
Across the mountains to the farthest lands.'

A group of monkeys went **EASTWARDS**
Another was **WESTWARD** bound
The third group marched **NORTHWARDS**
While the last group went all the way **SOUTH.**

Hanuman was in the group going south
His leader was a monkey called Angada
Along with them came the wise bear Jambavan
And other smart and powerful creatures.

For many days and nights they travelled
Inside small and **DARK CAVES** they looked
Into holes in the earth they peeped
At every passer-by they peered.

But nowhere could they find Sita
The missing princess of Ayodhya
'What will we tell our master?' they cried
'We have searched in every possible area.'

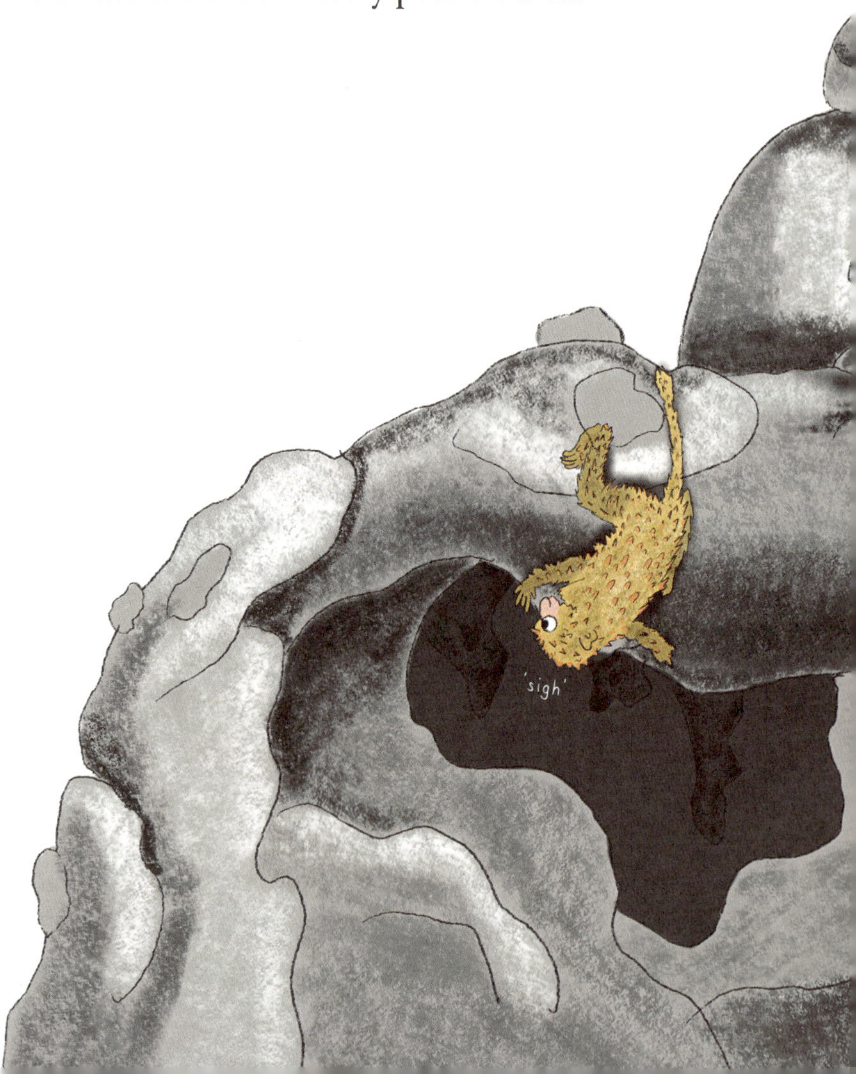

'HELLO?'
'HELLO?'
'sigh'

Just then the sharp and loud voice of an **EAGLE**
Called out to the monkey group
Seeing an eagle with its keen eyes and **BIG TALONS**
The monkeys feared he would eat them all.

'No! No! I will not eat you. Fearless you must be
I tell you I saw a monster carry Princess Sita to Lankapuri
Calling out, she was, to Rama and Lakshmana
Go across the ocean to the island and in Lanka you will be.'

'There in Lanka, dears
Find her you will
She is looking very frail and thin
Hurry, hurry,' he cried so shrill.

'Ah!' said the saddened monkeys
'Sita we have found
But how will we fly across an ocean
So deep and spread all around?'

'Lanka is about **1300 MILES AWAY**
And all the way and around is sea
None of us can fly across
We have a problem, don't you see?'

Then the wise **JAMBAVAN** stood up
'Rise my friend, Hanuman,' he said
'Have you your powers forgotten? You alone can do it
Just try, strong one, show us your **MIGHTY POWER**.'

Hanuman thought for a moment full
Yes, he could do it! For his dear Rama he would
He stood tall on a mountain high
And drew his breath in.

'Away I go to find Sita
Successful I will be!'
Resolving thus he leaped into the air
And off he went swoosh ahead.

'RISE!'
'STRONG HANUMAN'

A short while later, Hanuman felt
The sky was somewhat darker now
It is not night as yet, thought Hanuman
What is this that blocks my view?

A **MONSTER SURASA** by name
Stood ahead with her mouth open wide
'I have been waiting for you, little fellow,' she said
'To eat you is my will.'

GRRRR, she snarled
Ho ho ho, she laughed
She was looking forward to a tasty
Meal of the monkey, his tail and all.

'You can eat me,' said Hanuman
'But let me first do this job
Of finding Sita and telling Rama
Then I will be back. I give you my word.'

'Nothing doing! Enter my mouth right away
You can go no further, that is sure
My tummy is rumbling with hunger
I NEED TO EAT YOU NOW,' she roared.

Hanuman was not scared, brave as he was
He smiled to himself, he was thinking fast
'Open your mouth wider then,' he said
And grew to a bigger size to frighten her.

Surasa **OPENED HER MOUTH**
That now was very large
But Hanuman grew even larger and said,
'You are still not big enough!'

Surasa now opened her mouth even more
It covered a part of the sky
Hanuman grew so much bigger, oooh!
While to eat him Surasa tried and tried.

Then all of a sudden
In not even a second
Hanuman **SHRANK** and
Became the size of a fly.

Into Surasa's mouth he flew
And in a trice was out of it too
Before Surasa could close her mouth
Hanuman flew away, phew!

Thus the clever Hanuman
Fooled the monster Surasa
Then he went to **Lanka** to
FIND SITA, the mission he was on.

After hunting quite a bit
His master's wife Sita he found
For Hanuman always works hard to succeed
At whatever he sets his mind to.

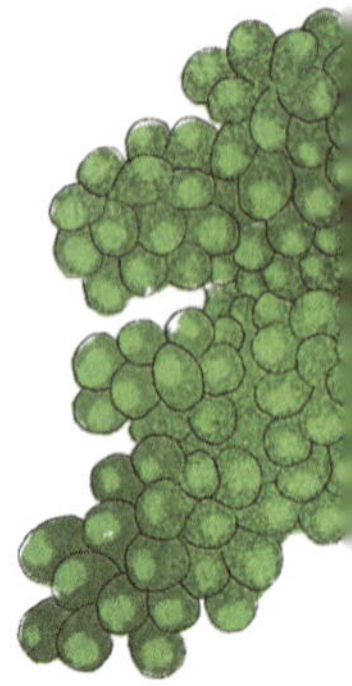

'sigh'
'sigh'

HANUMAN IN LANKA

Hanuman was flying to Lanka
ACROSS miles and **MILES OF SEA**
To search for Princess Sita
The wife of his master Rama was she.

The ten-headed monster Ravana
Had taken princess Sita away
'Ha ha ha,' had laughed Ravana, flexing his muscles
And all his ten heads had laughed gleefully too.

'No one can defeat me
A bird, a beast or even a god it may be
I am the best,' had guffawed Ravana
While the world hid in fear and anxiety.

Now where had Ravana taken Sita?
Where did his kingdom of Lanka lie?
To find that out many monkeys and bears
Roamed the world, upturning every stone and tree.

'Whoosh'
'Whoosh'

Hanuman had come southwards
Along with other monkeys and bears
He had **CROSSED THE OCEAN** to Lanka
Where Sita was said to be.

It was dark and the **MOON** was up
When Hanuman reaching Lanka sat on a treetop
'What a beautiful city I see
With so many gates and much security.'

'I think I should make myself small
So I won't be easily visible to all
Then flying into Lanka by night
I will see if Sita is anywhere in sight.'

Hanuman, now very small
Jumped and leaped on to the **BIG CITY WALL**
As he perched on the gate
A booming voice ordered him to wait.

'Who are you, O monkey!
Why do you enter the protected city?
Go back from where you came
I am Lankini, the guardian of this gate.'

'I am a visitor,' said Hanuman. 'I've come to see Lanka city
I will take a tour and leave in a jiffy
Just let me pass, kind lady
I will cause no trouble to any.'

‘Of course you cannot pass,’
Bellowed the **LADY, FEARSOME** and **HUGE**
‘Go back! Away you go
Or fight me, you naughty fellow.’

With his left arm, Hanuman moved her aside
And Lankini could not even that much bear
‘Oh! You are very strong though tiny, dear monkey
Please go and see what you want to,’ she said weakly.

'OHHHH!'

Thanking her, Hanuman went into the city bright
Lanka was indeed such a delight!
He saw coloured gems on **TALL PALACES**
And gold domes, lush gardens and open spaces.

And then he saw an **AMAZING AIRCRAFT**
Called the Pushpakavimana
Board it and it will take you
Wherever you wish to go.

Hanuman then entered Ravana's palace
Guarded by soldiers on elephants and horses
Tiny as he was, no one noticed him
In he went, softly, barely breathing.

It was past midnight and everyone was sleeping
Hanuman tiptoed into Ravana's home in a hush
Here he saw a lady snoring gently
And there another dreaming happily.

Then he saw **RAVANA SLEEPING** on a high bed
He looked so majestic, dressed as he was in red
Even as he was breathing heavily in slumber
Amazed Hanuman took a step back in terror.

'OHH!'
'Zzz'
'Zzzz'
'Zzzzzzz'

But Sita, he could still not see
Into every house he went and searched fully
'Oh dear, what shall I do?' thought Hanuman, a little sad
'I will not give up. I must find her,' he declared.

Making such a promise to himself
Hanuman wondered where else to search
All that was left was a garden of flowers, the Ashoka vana
'She will be there, I am sure,' he thought.

Jumping and excited he ran all the way
And in the garden, under a tree, he saw
A lady, **SAD** and **LONELY**. Thought Hanuman,
'Could that be Sita? It looks like her indeed.'

'Zzz'
'Zzz'
'zzz'

Surrounding her were many **MONSTERS**
Of different shapes and sizes, colours and features
Hanuman waited for all of them to fall asleep
And then told Sita that he had come in search of her.

Sita was delighted to see Hanuman
'But are you sure you come from Rama?'
She asked. 'Yes,' said Hanuman and gave her
The ring that Rama had sent through him.

In return Sita gave him her hairpin
'Take this to Rama with my love,' she said
'Tell him to come to Lanka quick and wage a war
Against the ten-headed King Ravana.'

By now the monsters had all woken up
And in groups to **FIGHT HANUMAN** they came
Oh dear, there were so many of them, angry and fierce
But Hanuman single-handedly fended them all off.

No one could match his strength
They all fled away in fear
Except for Ravana's brave son Meghnad
Who tied him up, our Hanuman dear.

Meghnad took Hanuman to his father Ravana
Who was growling with anger towards Hanuman
He had been waiting to see the monkey
Who had defeated everybody.

Hanuman now saw that King Ravana was good-looking
Tall and broad with muscles big
He was as well read as he was powerful
And had a smile so charming as well.

Ravana had made a mistake
He had troubled Sita and brought her away
And that was not fair in any way
If he had apologised, it would still have been OK.

'Even now if you say sorry to Rama
He will forgive you and let you go
When the wise ones make a mistake,' Hanuman said
'They feel sorry and correct it. Will you too?'

Ravana was not willing to say sorry
He was so **FULL OF FURY**
'Punish that monkey,' he roared
To all the **MINISTERS** of his court.

'PUNISH HIM!'
'thud'
'thump'

All the monsters of the city
Came eagerly forward to do just that
But Hanuman was so quick and clever
That he outsmarted them all, whoever.

When they tied him up
He became even smaller
So the ropes fell off
And Hanuman leaped away.

When they tried to shoot an **ARROW**
At Hanuman, he flew into the sky
And when they shot into the sky
He threw a **HUGE ROCK** their way.

Frightened and in a panic
They all ran away
Ravana then tried to hurt him
By tying burning rags to Hanuman's tail.

What no one knew was that Hanuman was blessed
By the mighty fire god himself
Unhurt he was, and unafraid
He flew all over Lanka setting everything **ABLAZE**.

Then, **WHOOSH**, he took off from Lanka
And across the sea he flew to Rama
'Seen her!' he exclaimed giving Rama the good news
Of having found Sita in Ravana's land.

'Now we have to quickly go to Lanka,
To rescue Princess Sita and teach Ravana
That courage means admitting your mistake
Squarely and making amends,' said Hanuman.

So Rama, his brother Lakshmana
And all the monkeys and bears
Got ready to leave for Lanka
And bring Sita safely back home.

ABOUT THE STORIES

Here is a little note to acquaint the adult reader with the context of the stories of Hanuman. It is hoped that once the context is known, a sense of belonging to the great tradition will be established, and one can read/tell the stories to children with a greater sense of authority.

The three stories that appear in this book are from the Ramayana, one of the most loved epics of India. The Ramayana was originally written by a sage named Valmiki. It is divided into six kandas or sections, with the Uttara kanda, which is something like an epilogue, being the seventh. Rama, the prince of Ayodhya, is the hero of the story, while Ravana, the king of Lanka, is the villain. When Rama, his wife, Sita, and brother Lakshmana are exiled to live in the forest, Ravana sees Rama as a threat to his status and power. To harass Rama, who is far stronger than him, Ravana kidnaps Sita. Rama is distraught and embarks on a search for Sita. That is when he meets Sugriva, the monkey king of Kishkinda, and his minister Hanuman. Hanuman is one of the most charming characters of the Ramayana not only because he possesses immense strength, great intellect, courage, fearlessness, wisdom and a felicity with words but also because of his great loyalty to Rama.

HOW HANUMAN GOT HIS NAME

The story of how Hanuman got his name appears in cantos 35 and 36 of the Uttara kanda. Rama tells Sage Agastya that but for Hanuman and Sugriva he would not have been able to defeat Ravana and rescue Sita. Describing Hanuman, he says:

Shauryam dakshyam balam dhairyam pragyata nayasadhanam
Vikramashch prabhavashch hanumaiti kritalaya

Valour, competence, strength, fortitude, wisdom, diplomacy
Heroic power and radiance seem to have taken residence in Hanuman

'How is it that Hanuman is endowed with so many qualities?' asks Rama of Sage Agastya. Then the sage tells Rama the story of how Hanuman was born and how he got his name and his many powers. The story is also touched upon in the Kishkinda kanda, the fourth kanda of the Ramayana, chapter 66, verses 21, 22, 23 and 24. Here Jambavan, a bear who is another minister in Sugriva's cabinet, reminds Hanuman of all the powers the gods had bestowed on him when he was a baby. The planet that came to peer at Hanuman's face was Rahu, described in Hindu texts as a shadow planet and as the king of meteors.

HOW HANUMAN CROSSED THE SEA

While Ravana is carrying Sita away from the forest, Jatayu, an eagle friend of Rama's, tries to stop him. But Ravana proves too strong for him. Rama returns to his ashrama and is shocked when he does not find Sita. The brothers, Rama and Lakshmana, set out in search of Sita. Rama meets with the monkey king of Kishkinda, Sugriva, and his minister Hanuman. When Sugriva hears of Sita's abduction, he promises to help in the search and assigns different directions to different groups of the monkeys and bears. This appears in the last few chapters of the Kishkinda kanda. They all leave accordingly. Much hope is placed on Hanuman, who is with the south-bound team. They search everywhere but cannot find Sita and become despondent. Then Sampati, Jatayu's brother, informs them that he had seen Ravana carrying Sita away and that she is in Lanka. Hanuman leaps into the sky and after an encounter with Surasa over the sea reaches Lankapuri, or Lanka.

Uthishta harishardula lakyasva maharnavam
Para hi sarva bhootanaam Hanumanya gatistava

Get up you, the most powerful one, and cross the ocean
Of all creatures in the world, you are the fastest

The following verse, which is evocative of Hanuman's firm resolve, is the first shloka of the Sundara kanda (chapter 1, verse 1):

Tatho Ravananitayaha Sitayaha Shatrukrishnaha
Iyesha Padma anveshtum Charanacharite Pathi

Then to search for Sita who had been led away by Ravana
Hanuman decided to travel through the skies (the path of the
charanas or celestial bards)

HANUMAN GOES TO LANKA

On reaching Lanka, Hanuman begins searching for Sita there. This story is told in the Sundara kanda, the fifth kanda. Hanuman feels dejected when his search for Sita yields nothing. Then he motivates himself with a very powerful verse (Sundara kanda, chapter 12, verse 10):

Anirvedaha shriyo moolam anirvedaha param sukham
Anirvedo hi satatam sarva artheshu pravratakaha
Karoti safalam jantoho karma yaktatkaroti saha

Warding off depression is essential for prosperity and critical for happiness
To keep away depression is essential to carry out any activity, at any time
It will bring success to any endeavour that a man takes on

The verse where Hanuman reports to Rama that he has seen Sita is well known (Sundara kanda, chapter 64, verse 43). Hanuman's opening words are that he has seen Sita, thereby communicating the core of his message clearly and without delay. This saves Rama from wondering what news Hanuman had brought, good or otherwise.

Drishta Devi iti Haumat vadanamritapamam
Aakarnaya vachanam ramo harshamapa salakshmanaha

'Seen Sita!' These words of Hanuman, sweet as nectar they were
These touching words made Rama and Lakshmana very happy

Once they know where Sita is, Rama, Lakshmana, Sugriva, Hanuman and all the monkeys and bears go to Lanka and wage a war against Ravana and his army. Rama emerges victorious and Sita is rescued. After the war, they all return to Ayodhya, where Rama is crowned king.

ABOUT THE AUTHOR

Author and translator Sudhamahi Regunathan's books include *Rishabhayan: The Story of the First King*, *The Colours of Desire on the Canvas of Restraint: The Jaina Way* and *Taken Away: The Life of an Ordinary Monk*, co-authored with a Buddhist monk. Her interest lies in understanding different faiths and beliefs. A former vice chancellor, Sudhamahi writes for adults and children. Her most recent book for children is *Ramayana for Babies.*

ABOUT THE ILLUSTRATOR

Anushka Madhavan is an illustrator and designer of children's books based in Chennai. Among the many books she has illustrated are *Jacklin and Amali* by The Banyan Foundation and *Would You Rather: Ocean or Space* by Shaili Shah. She also conducts workshops in colleges and schools on the art of bookmaking. She is passionate about books, art and designing.

COMING SOON

BOOK 2

HANUMAN ACHIEVES THE IMPOSSIBLE

HANUMAN CARRIES A MOUNTAIN   HANUMAN IN KADALI FOREST

HANUMAN THE GREAT MUSICIAN

8